SOPHIE
The Show-off

Home Farm Twins

Sophie
The Show-off

Jenny Oldfield

Illustrated by Kate Aldous

Hodder
Children's
Books

a division of Hodder Headline plc

A Catalogue record for this book is available from the British Library

ISBN 0 340 69987 6

Typeset by Avon Dataset Ltd, Bidford-on-Avon, Warks

Printed and bound in Great Britain by
Mackays of Chatham plc, Chatham, Kent

Hodder Children's Books
a division of Hodder Headline plc
338 Euston Road
London NW1 3BH

One

'Her name is Sood Sawaat Chaem Choi!' Luke Martin said proudly.

'Sood – what?' Helen Moore asked.

Luke's new Siamese cat sat on the window-sill outside the village shop. Her fur was smooth and creamy, and she had a black face and ears and the most amazing bright blue eyes.

'Sood Sawaat Chaem Choi. It means Dearest Sweet Lady.'

'In what language?' Hannah sat beside Helen on a wooden bench gazing up at the graceful cat. She loved its dainty feet, its long legs and tapering

1

black tail with the kink at the end.

Sood Sawaat Chaem Choi opened her mouth and yowled.

'In the Thai language,' Luke explained. 'Thailand used to be called Siam. All Siamese cats are descended from the king's cats that lived in the palace at Bangkok.'

'They *look* like royal cats,' Helen agreed.

'Proud,' Hannah added. 'As if they know how beautiful they are.'

Sood Sawaat Chaem Choi lifted her haughty, wedge-shaped head and stared down at them through half-closed eyes.

'The King of Siam made an order that no one else in the land was allowed to keep these cats, and the palace guards kept watch over his own cats night and day.' Luke enjoyed telling the twins about the history of the glamorous breed. He stood in the doorway of his shop, arms folded, gazing fondly at his cat as she sat in the sun.

'Are you going to say all those names when you call her in for tea?' Hannah asked doubtfully. To her it sounded a terrible mouthful.

'Like, "Here, Sood-Sawaat-Thingy-Thingy!" ' Helen

called in a high, 'Here, Tiddles!' type of voice. She giggled and nudged Hannah off the edge of the bench.

Luke coughed. 'I call her Sophie for short.'

Sophie stood up on the window-sill, arched her back and hissed at the twins.

'Don't take any notice,' Luke assured Helen and Hannah. His bearded face beamed from ear to ear, his brown eyes twinkled. There was no stopping him now that he'd started on his favourite subject. 'Siamese cats are really devoted, loyal and friendly animals. They make brilliant family pets because they're so intelligent and loving.'

'We only called in for a bag of crisps!' Helen whispered to Hannah, munching hungrily. They were on their way back to Home Farm after a hard day at school.

'Yes, but she's a pretty amazing cat,' Hannah had to admit.

'She's OK,' Helen said grudgingly, half under her breath, but loud enough for the cat to hear.

Sophie swished her long, tapering tail back and forth. She glared at Helen with her brilliant blue eyes.

'They show all the loving affection of a dog,' Luke announced, as if he was reading from a guide to Siamese cats. He reached out his hand to stroke his beautiful pet.

Sophie swiped out with a front paw, ears flat, tail still swishing.

'Yeah!' Helen said, rapidly standing up and taking a step back.

'They have the courage of a lion,' Luke recited. '. . . The grace of a panther.'

Sophie balanced along the window-sill, stretched out to sniff at the cheese and onion crisps in Helen's packet . . . and promptly fell off the edge.

'Yeah!' Hannah laughed. She watched Sophie land upright on the pavement and catch sight of the tabby cat from next door who was sunning himself under the bench.

'And the speed of a deer!' Luke declared.

Sophie chased the tabby along the pavement, on to a higgledy-piggledy stone wall, over the flowering blackberry bushes and up the long field behind the shop.

'Wow!' Helen and Hannah said. Both were genuinely impressed. The Siamese cat had soon overtaken Tabs. She streaked ahead on her muscular legs, her lithe, sleek body speeding through the long grass.

'Nought to sixty miles per hour in five seconds!' Helen laughed.

Tubby Tabs struggled along behind.

Then, suddenly, unexpectedly, Sophie stopped. In a milli-second she did a backwards flip and landed on stiff legs, facing next door's cat.

'She's a cross between a racing-car and an acrobat!' Hannah breathed.

'Or a race horse and a gymnast!' Helen echoed.

'Here, Sophie!' Luke called. 'They're very, very clever creatures!' he insisted, climbing the wall after her. 'Much more intelligent than your common-or-garden moggy!'

Sophie squared up to Tabs, ready for a scrap.

'She's only playing,' Luke said hastily. 'You can actually train them to come when you call.' He strode up the field. 'Here, Sophie! Come here, girl!'

The Siamese cat ignored him. She had her pretend fight with Tabs, swiping out with her paws, hissing and arching her back. Then, soon bored, she twitched the kinked tip of her tail and skittered off through the grass.

The twins stood at the wall and watched Luke give chase. As the Siamese cat reached the nearest beech tree and sprang up it, Helen finished munching her crisps. 'What do you think?'

'Of Sood Sawaat Thingy-Thingy?' Hannah sighed happily.

'Sweetest Dear Lady. Dearest Sweet Lady.' Helen could still hear Luke calling for his cat. Sophie crouched, just out of reach. As Luke reached up on tiptoe, she stood, pirouetted and stepped away like a tightrope-walker along the smooth branch.

'I think she's really beautiful!' Hannah sighed. She pictured a Siamese cat at Home Farm, along with Socks, their own tabby cat, and Solo their grey pony, and the geese, the rabbits, the hens . . .

As Luke jumped up to reach the branch, Sophie chose her moment. The cat jumped with one smooth, easy movement straight on to Luke's shoulder, on to the grass, and away again.

Helen smiled. 'Beautiful, but a bit of a show-off,' she decided, stuffing her empty crisp packet into her schoolbag and heading for home.

* * *

'Read my lips!' Mary Moore laughed over breakfast next morning. 'N-O, No!'

'But, Mu-um!' Hannah and Helen chorused.

Hannah had chosen her moment carefully. The sun was shining in through the kitchen doorway, the early morning chores were done, and their mum was humming a tune as she got ready for work.

'Can we have a Siamese cat?' Hannah had asked. No point beating about the bush.

'No "buts"!' Mary warned. Glancing in the mirror in the hallway, she brushed her long, dark hair back from her tanned face. 'This place is overflowing with animals as it is.'

She stepped over Speckle, the twins' Border collie, who lay across the doorstep. Out in the flagged yard, brown hens pecked grain from between the cracks. They ignored Socks, the young tabby cat with white paws, who crouched in the barn doorway, ready to pounce.

'Dad?' Hannah turned to David Moore for support. 'What do you think? Wouldn't it be wonderful to have a teenie-weenie, well-behaved, gorgeous Siamese cat?'

His grey eyes twinkled. 'Aren't those the cats with the grace of the panther . . . the speed of the deer?'

Hannah frowned. 'You've been talking to Luke!'

'Last night,' he confessed. 'I couldn't get a word in edgeways. We were supposed to be picking the cricket team for the match this Saturday, but all Luke could think about was his blessed cat!'

'Well, wouldn't it?' Hannah persisted, dolloping marmalade on to her toast.

Her mum reached over her head to pick up her car keys. 'N-O, No!' she said again.

'It looks like you'll have to make do with visiting Luke,' her dad said. 'Do some cat-sitting for him while we mow the cricket pitch grass this evening.'

'She's a first class pedigree cat,' Luke told the twins. He was fitting a dainty red leather harness around Sophie's shoulders and fastening it under her chest. 'That's why she has such a posh official name.'

'So how come she ended up at the cat sanctuary?' Helen asked.

The twins had driven down from Home Farm with their dad to do what he'd suggested. While the men cut the grass and rolled the pitch, ready for an important cricket match in ten days' time, they would look after Sophie.

'I'm not sure exactly.' Luke fitted a lead to the harness. The Siamese cat was going for a walk. 'All I know is that I dropped in by chance on Lucy Carlton at Stonelea, and there she was, large as life and twice as beautiful.'

'Had she been abandoned?' Hannah asked.

'I don't even know that. She's ten months old and she used to live in Nesfield. That's all I found out.'

'Are we ready?' David Moore wanted to get started. 'It'll be dark before we even begin at this rate.'

So they set off up the road from Luke's shop, past the rows of terraced stone houses that lined the main village street, to the smooth, open expanse of Doveton Cricket Club.

'Look at that!' passers-by exclaimed, leaning out of their cars in admiration. 'A cat on a lead!'

Sophie picked up her dainty feet and trotted along, good as gold. Hannah held the lead tight.

'Isn't that sweet?' Old ladies stood at their garden gates and exclaimed. 'So well-behaved.'

The cat held her head up, high-stepping towards the cricket ground.

'. . . Showing off!' Helen muttered under her breath. She wasn't nearly so impressed by Sood Sawaat Thingy as Hannah was. She preferred normal, everyday moggies like Socks and Tabs. Or like Sinbad, Miss Wesley's fluffy black cat.

'*Yee-owwwl*!' Sophie spotted Sinbad; a black dot at the far side of the cricket ground. She jerked the lead out of Hannah's hand and shot under the gate.

Helen put her hands to her ears to shut out the

terrible yowling noise. Hannah made a dive for the trailing lead and missed.

'Sophie, come back!' Luke opened the gate and gave chase.

Across the field, Sinbad arched his back and swished his tail, ready for anything.

Sophie howled and charged. She flew across the velvet-smooth wicket.

' "Swift as a cheetah",' David Moore remarked, leaning on the gate in resigned amusement.

'You're quoting Luke again,' Helen grumbled. Sinbad stood his ground until the very last second, then suddenly turned and vanished under a hedge.

'Yes, but it's true,' her dad insisted.

Hannah picked herself up from the ground. In the distance, Luke waved his arms and shouted for his cat. Sophie stalked along the hedge, calling out a warning to Sinbad not to return. She carried herself like a queen in a royal palace, looking down on her humble subjects. When Luke came within arm's length, she casually put on a burst of speed, then stalked on.

'He's got his hands full with that cat,' the twins' dad smiled, going to unlock the mower from the hut round the back of the pavilion.

The low sun cast long shadows across the perfect pitch. Luke trailed after Sophie, calling her name in vain.

'He has,' Helen agreed. She watched the Siamese cat suddenly duck her head and roll on to her side.

'Now she wants to play!' Hannah gasped. Forgetting that she'd charged across his precious pitch, Luke went down on to his hands and knees to tickle her. 'She can wind him round her little fin . . . paw!'

One thing Luke had said was true, Helen realised. Sophie was a very clever animal. 'She's trouble!' she warned. Beautiful and clever. 'Big, big trouble!'

Sophie climbed into Luke's arms and purred as she gazed up at him with her big blue eyes.

Two

'Keep your fingers crossed and hope that it doesn't rain,' David Moore told the twins as he dropped them off the following Saturday at Stonelea Cat Sanctuary.

He was dressed in a white shirt, pullover and trousers, ready for a cricket match; Doveton versus Nesfield. Doveton was playing away this week, in the build-up to a return match on home ground next weekend.

'Good luck!' Helen called. She stood by the gate, under the sanctuary sign of a black cat. As she glanced up, she felt a fine, warm drizzle fall on to her face.

'Hope you win!' Hannah waved her dad off. She gazed up towards Hardstone Pass, where the clouds had gathered, then down the valley towards Lake Rydal. The little town of Nesfield, strung out along the shore, was still in bright sunlight. Perhaps the cricket teams would be lucky with the weather after all.

'Oh, and remember what your mum said!' Their dad stopped the car and leaned out.

'That we could visit Miss Carlton . . .' Helen began.

'. . . As long as we weren't a nuisance,' Hannah finished for her.

'You've got it! Look but don't touch. In other words, enjoy yourselves, but don't even *think* about bringing another stray cat home with you!' He waved cheerily and chugged on down the hill.

'As if we would!' Hannah grinned. She turned towards the cottage tucked against the steep side of Rydal Fell, nestling by a clear, splashing waterfall, with ivy and climbing roses intertwined up the rough slate walls. And, of course, there were the cats.

A pure white cat sat in a tree, a fat grey cat sipped milk from a saucer on the doorstep. A tortoiseshell led three black, brown and white patched kittens across the path in single file.

'We're only here to find out more about Sophie,' Helen insisted. 'We promised Luke we would!'

'Who are we trying to kid?' Hannah sighed. If she could, she would give every single stray cat in Lucy Carlton's sanctuary a home.

'There you are!' Miss Carlton herself squeezed past the grey cat on the doorstep. She was a tiny, thin old woman with stiff joints and a slight stoop. Her voice was soft, her pointed face smiling under a neat cap of curly white hair.

Helen and Hannah said hello, as more cats appeared from beneath bushes in the overgrown garden. They came and twined themselves around the girls' legs, rubbing their heads against their ankles, purring loudly. One had a broad white face marked with old battle scars and a badly-chewed ear. Helen picked him up and stroked him.

'Hmm!' Miss Carlton tutted and shook her head. 'Old Tipsy gets the sympathy vote every time!'

The battered cat purred like a car engine in Helen's arms.

'Everyone feels sorry for him because he looks as

if he's been in the wars,' the old lady explained. 'He gets more fussing than the rest of my cats put together.'

'What about Sophie?' Hannah asked, turning to the reason for their visit. 'Did visitors like her?'

'Ah, you mean Sood Sawaat Chaem Choi?' The moment Lucy Carlton sat in a garden seat, two cats climbed on to her lap. 'The elegant Seal Point Siamese. Yes, she was a lovely creature.' She stroked the cats who had made themselves at home. 'But people didn't necessarily take to her; perhaps because she was too . . . well, too downright beautiful!'

'How do you mean?' Helen sat on the grass with Tipsy, the war-torn hero.

'That cat was close to perfection as far as looks go,' Miss Carlton explained. 'But perfection can be offputting, don't you think? You can't sympathize with it.'

Hannah's puzzled frown lifted. 'That's right. Sophie looks too perfect to be real!'

The old lady nodded, then sighed. 'Her life before she came here had been far from perfect, however.'

'Why? Where did you find her?' Helen grew more interested. Sophie's past obviously had a darker side.

'I didn't find her; the police did.' Miss Carlton pursed her lips, then went on with the story. 'It was in February this year. We'd had a couple of very cold weeks, and someone rang the police station to say they could hear a cat miaowing inside a deserted house just off the market square in Nesfield. According to a neighbour, the owner, Mr Lewis, had locked up the house and gone to Spain at the end of January.'

'And left the cat without food?' Hannah cried. 'In the cold and dark?'

The old lady nodded. 'The neighbour didn't even

17

know Mr Lewis owned a cat. Apparently he'd had her since October and never once let her out into the garden.'

'What did the police do?' Helen prompted. She pushed her hair behind her ears and stared intently at Miss Carlton.

'They broke into the house.'

'How?'

'They had to kick down the door, I believe. At first they couldn't find the cat, though the whole place smelled terrible, as you can imagine. There wasn't a scrap of food, but the tap in the bathroom sink was dripping, and it's my bet that that was the reason Sophie survived.'

'By drinking water from the tap?' Hannah was horrified. She spoke in a quiet, shaky voice.

'How could anyone do that?' Helen felt angry with this Mr Lewis. 'Where did the police find Sophie in the end?'

'Under the bed, too frightened and weak to come out. She tried to bite the policeman, but he wore a pair of gloves to protect his hands. It wasn't long before he had hold of her and brought her straight here.'

'Was she starving?' Hannah whispered.

'Too weak to stand, trembling from head to toe and so thin her ribs stuck out. She was only about six months old and weighed hardly anything. I couldn't feed her big meals at first; only small ones until gradually she got over her terrible experience.'

'Home alone!' Helen frowned.

'But she must have cost this Mr Lewis loads of money,' Hannah pointed out. 'Couldn't he afford to put her in a cattery when he went on holiday?'

Miss Carlton nodded. 'No doubt he just couldn't be bothered. He went to all the expense of buying a pedigree Siamese cat and giving her a grand name, but was too selfish to look after her properly. Some people are like that, believe me.'

'Sophie could've died!' Helen cried. She tried to imagine her thin and scraggy, close to starvation. 'What happened to Mr Lewis?'

'The last I heard, which was a couple of months ago, he was still living in his house in Spain. The police couldn't do anything until he came back to Britain.'

'I hope they put him in prison!' Hannah said

fiercely. 'So did you change her name from Sood Sawaat . . . ?'

'. . . Chaem Choi.' Miss Carlton nodded. 'Well, it was much too much of a mouthful for a little scrap of a thing.'

'Sophie suits her much better.' Helen put Tipsy down and stood up. 'Though, now that she's better and looking good again, she does seem to have grown more snobby.'

'You've noticed that, have you?' Miss Carlton gave a little smile. 'Do you think there's a touch of the show-off in her nature?'

'Yes!' Helen said smartly.

'No!' Hannah wouldn't hear a word said against Sophie, especially now that she knew her sad past.

'They are rather fussy cats,' the old lady confirmed. 'They groom themselves much more thoroughly than the likes of Tipsy. That's why their coats gleam and glow with health. And of course, they have that peculiar miaow.'

'Uh!' Helen put her hands to her ears as she imagined Sophie's yowling cry.

'I like it!' Hannah insisted.

'Every Siamese cat has a different personality,'

Lucy Carlton went on. Her thin hands stroked the soft fur of the two tabby cats on her lap. 'The Seal Points – ones like Sophie with almost black faces, legs and so on – are often the most friendly and outgoing.'

'See!' Hannah turned to Helen to prove her point.

'But poor Sophie had lost her trust in human nature when she first came to Stonelea. Even now she can be rather stand-offish.'

Helen returned Hannah's knowing look.

'I remember how she lorded it over Tipsy.' The good-natured owner of the cat sanctuary laughed. 'She would glide by, nose in the air, and ignore all his efforts to be friends. Then she would turn round and steal the food from his dish without a second thought!'

'Would Tipsy let her?' Helen looked again at the stocky, bow-legged tomcat as he strolled across the lawn.

'Oh yes. He was head over heels in love with her!' Miss Carlton laughed again. 'It broke his heart when Luke Martin came by and decided to give her a home.'

'Why did Luke choose her?' Hannah asked.

The old lady gave the twins a bright, knowing look. 'I blame those blue eyes,' she confided. 'Luke said they made her look sweet and innocent.But we see beyond the sparkling eyes, don't we girls? Sweet and innocent! Little did Luke know when he took her back to Doveton that Sophie would be anything but!'

Three

'Be gentle with your dad when he gets up this morning,' Mary Moore told Hannah and Helen early next day.

'Why?' Helen had arrived back from a walk up the fell with Speckle. She hung his lead on the hook on the back of the kitchen door.

'Doveton lost the cricket match. His face is still so long his chin's practically hitting the floor!' As usual, she was in a rush to set off for work. The Curlew, her cafe in Nesfield, was always busy on a sunny Sunday. 'Extra milk, clean tea-towels, fresh flowers for the tables.' She ran through a list of the things she needed to take.

Hannah helped her carry them to the car. 'We'll try and cheer dad up,' she promised.

'Apparently the great defeat has something to do with a bowler called Dennis in the Nesfield team.' Mary stacked the tea-towels on the back seat. 'I don't pretend to understand the finer points of cricket, but from what I can gather, your dad and Luke are convinced that this Dennis did something illegal to the ball before he bowled.'

'He probably rubbed dirt into it to make it spin funny,' Hannah said casually.

Her mum looked at her in surprise. 'How do you know that?'

'I hear the kids at school talk about it.'

'Whatever.' Mary shrugged and got into the car. 'I expect your dad will want to go down to the village later this morning to talk over the painful details with Luke.'

Hannah's eyes lit up. A picture of Sophie sitting on the shop window-sill flashed into her head. 'We'll go with him!' she decided.

At half past eight, David Moore shuffled downstairs.

His wavy hair fell over his forehead, his blue T-shirt was crumpled and creased.

'I've fed the animals and walked Speckle!' Helen greeted him with a big mug of steaming-hot tea.

'And I've groomed Solo and arranged to go for a ride with Laura and Sultan later this afternoon,' Hannah told him. The twins knew that Laura too was always up early. She lived at Doveton Manor on the road into the village.

'Uh-uh-uh!' their dad groaned. 'I'm stiff all over from yesterday's match.'

'Never mind, it's a brilliant, sunny day.' Helen knew this wasn't like her bumbling, happy-go-lucky dad. Yesterday's defeat must really have got him down.

'Uh!' He reached for the newspaper and hid his face behind it.

'Luke rang,' Hannah said quietly.

'What? When? Why didn't you wake me up?' David sprang into action. He dropped the paper and scrambled for his car keys. 'Come on. What are we waiting for?'

'I'm absolutely sure that Dennis tampered with the

ball!' Luke claimed from inside the shop.

Helen and Hannah sat on the bench outside, tempting Sophie on to their laps with her favourite cheese and onion crisps.

'Dennis the Menace!' Helen grinned.

'Yes, but we couldn't prove it,' David Moore sighed. 'We lost the match by five runs, all because of his dirty tricks!'

Sophie jumped neatly from her favourite spot on the window-sill to the bench. Her long whiskers brushed Hannah's arm as she leaned forward to take a crisp from Helen. She crunched it between her sharp, pointed teeth.

'We'll have to make sure it doesn't happen again next Saturday, when their team comes here,' Luke decided. 'I've got half an hour to spare before I open up shop, so let's trim and roll that pitch until it's absolutely flat. There won't be a mark on it. And then, if the ball doesn't bounce properly, we'll know that it's Dennis up to his tricks!'

'And this time we'll prove it to the umpires!' The twins' dad sounded determined and businesslike again. Talking to Luke had done the trick.

The two cricket fanatics came out of the shop

together. 'Keep Sophie out of mischief for me,' Luke said to Helen and Hannah. 'We won't be long.'

The twins nodded. Sophie was so busy crunching crisps that she allowed Helen to pick her up and carry her inside.

'Good idea. Try to make sure she stays in,' David Moore told them as he and Luke headed for the cricket field. 'That should keep her out of trouble while we're away.'

'Famous last words!' Helen muttered.

Sophie had climbed on to the top shelf behind Luke's counter. She sat way out of reach, next to a wobbly jar full of jelly-babies.

'Trouble should be her middle name,' Hannah agreed. 'Never mind Sood Sawaat-Thingy!'

The cat sniffed at the tempting jar of sweets and tapped it with her paw.

'Uh-ohh!' Helen breathed, craning her neck and staring up at the unsafe jar.

Hannah got into position directly underneath, as Sophie sat on her haunches and wrapped both front legs around it.

The cat nudged the jar closer to the edge of the

shelf. 'Watch out!' Helen cried.

The jar teetered on the brink. Sophie sniffed at the lid, tempted by the sugary smell. She nudged it one last time.

'Here it comes!' Helen warned.

The jar of jelly-babies plunged from the shelf. Hannah held out her arms to catch it.

'Butter-fingers!' Helen yelled as she missed.

The glass jar hit the floor and smashed. The sweets scattered everywhere. From the high shelf, Sophie yowled and cried.

'Quick, fetch a dustpan and brush!' Hannah looked in dismay at the broken glass. 'We mustn't let Sophie cut her paws!' She stood guard as Helen ran to Luke's store-room for the brush.

'What's Luke gonna say?' Helen moaned as she went down on her hands and knees and began to sweep up the mess. 'He trusted us to keep Sophie out of trouble.'

'She didn't realise what she was doing.' Hannah made excuses. 'How could she be expected to know that glass would break?' Anxiously she watched the Siamese cat jump smoothly from the shelf to the counter, and prepare to leap again.

'Don't let her get out!' Helen warned. She was crouched with the dustpan and brush underneath Sophie's launching place.

Too late. The cat jumped over her head towards the door. A flick of her long tail, and she was gone.

'Let's leave this!' Hannah gasped, pointing at the debris on the floor. She scrambled out of the door after Sophie, in time to see her heading down the footpath that led to Doveton Lake. 'We'd better fetch her before Luke comes back.'

So they locked the shop door and ran, knowing that Sophie was fast and agile. If she wanted to, she could easily outrun them, or hide high in the branches of a tree.

'There she is!' Helen spotted the cat's blue eyes gazing out at them from a clump of forget-me-not flowers in the garden of a house that overlooked the lake.

Sophie let them come close, then she jumped straight up into the air and landed stiff-legged. She twirled round and ran on to the pebbly beach.

'This isn't funny!' Hannah scolded. The cat obviously wanted to play.

'She thinks this is hide-and-seek,' Helen muttered.

Sophie had snuck into another garden; this time the one belonging to their teacher, Miss Wesley. Helen recognised the white gate and the sign that said 'Lakeside Cottage'.

'*Mee-oww*!' A loud cry came from the garden.

Helen stared at Hannah. 'Sinbad!'

'*Yee-owwl*!' Sophie replied.

The twins reached the hedge and peered over. There were Sinbad and Sophie face to face by Miss Wesley's stone bird-bath, backs arched, fur standing on end. Sinbad flattened his ears and hissed: *This is my territory*! Sophie lashed her tail back and forth.

'She's for it this time!' Hannah groaned. The teacher's spirited black cat looked more than a match for the dainty Siamese.

Perhaps Sophie knew it. She turned away from Sinbad and slowly, deliberately walked to the far side of the bird-bath.

'It's like she's moving in slow motion!' Helen whispered. 'Now she's rolling on to her side, look!'

'She's telling Sinbad she wants to play.' Hannah gasped at Sophie's cheek.

'He's falling for it!' Helen watched Sinbad smooth himself out and follow Sophie. 'Yes, he's definitely making friends!'

Sinbad walked all the way round the playful visitor, warily at first, then ducking his head and rolling beside her. Soon, the two cats were the best of friends.

'Let's try and grab her,' Hannah suggested. She clicked the latch on the gate and pushed it open.

Helen glanced at the cottage where Miss Wesley lived. The windows were open, but there was no sign of their teacher. Holding her breath, she followed Hannah into the garden.

Sophie heard the twins approach. She gave a

sideways glance at the two clumsy, crouching figures. Her pointed ears flicked disdainfully. *Let's go!*

Sinbad agreed. He set off with Sophie across the lawn, streaking between Helen and Hannah and through the open gate on to the pebble beach. The cats darted between the legs of Sunday trippers, over upturned rowing-boats waiting by the shore, and along the gently lapping water's edge.

'Oh no!' Hannah shut her eyes in despair. The lake stretched out clear and smooth before them. Cats and water! Knowing Sophie, it wouldn't be long before *one* of them got wet.

Helen ran after them. Her feet crunched over the smooth grey pebbles, her dark hair flew back from her face.

But now Sophie was showing off. She knew that the twins would never catch up, and she knew she had an audience. *Watch me!* she invited, overtaking Sinbad, then performing her amazing backwards flip.

'Did you see that?' someone cried.

'Swee-eet!' a girl eating ice-cream cried, as Sophie raced Sinbad along the wooden jetty that stretched fifty metres into the lake. The girl was queuing with her parents for a ride in one of the steam-boats that were moored at the end.

'Sweet . . . I don't think so!' Helen muttered as she leaped on to the jetty after the cats. She could hear Hannah's footsteps clumping along after her.

'It's OK, we've cornered them!' Hannah gasped. The two cats had reached the end of the jetty and had nowhere else to go.

The captain of the first steam-boat rang a brass bell. He unhitched the mooring ropes and raised the gang-plank. Ten o'clock sharp; departure time for the fully loaded Doveton Belle.

Sophie skidded to a halt. She saw the boat drift free of the jetty, heard the engine chug then roar. There was a polished wooden rail around the sides of the old-fashioned boat. The gap between her and the rail could still be bridged . . .

'Sophie; no!' Helen cried.

Ready? Sophie turned to Sinbad. The eyes of the crowd were on her. With one magnificent bound, she launched herself.

'No!' Hannah hid her face in her hands.

Sophie flew through the air and made a perfect landing on the rail of the Doveton Belle.

Four

The steam-boat's captain cut the engine in astonishment. His passengers cried out.

'Did you see that?'

'Wasn't that amazing?'

'Watch out, here comes another!'

Hannah peeped through the gaps in her fingers. Sinbad crouched at the edge of the jetty, ready to jump.

The boat was drifting further out. It would take a miraculous leap.

Helen tried to stop the black cat. But Sophie had made it, so why shouldn't he? He gathered his courage, then sprang from the wooden platform.

'Ooh!'

'Aah!' The tourists on the boat jumped to their feet. The Doveton Belle rocked from side to side.

Sinbad's front paws touched the polished rail. He dug in his sharp claws. But at that split second, the Belle rocked away from the jetty. The cat hung on for dear life.

'He's going to make it!'

'No, he's not. He's slipping!'

'*Yeeowwl!*' Sophie encouraged Sinbad to hold tight. She balanced daintily on the rocking rail, back legs straight, tail up. Her head was down, peering over the edge at her vanishing friend.

'Cat overboard!' Helen cried.

Splash! Sinbad hit the cold, clear water. He sank like a stone.

There was a gasp, then everyone fell silent. A wavery, black shape was visible under the water. For a few seconds no one moved.

Then Helen kicked off her shoes. She ran and jumped, fully clothed. Another splash. This time it was her plunging into the lake.

Down she dropped. Great bubbles of air pushed

up through her shorts and T-shirt as she held her breath and opened her eyes. There in the silent, underwater world was a weird-looking Sinbad; head thrust back, eyes closed, and his long fur streaming around his face as he sank tail-first.

Helen kicked her legs and swam towards the drowning cat. She scooped her arms under him and aimed for the surface. The bright light of the sun beckoned her. Kicking hard, holding Sinbad close to her, she burst out of the water into the air.

'Well done!' the boat's captain cried when he saw that she'd saved the cat.

Passengers clapped, while Hannah knelt at the edge of the jetty, ready to take Sinbad back on to dry land. Helen handed him over, then turned and swam for the shore. That would teach him to copy Sophie, she thought sourly. She waded on to the pebbles and turned to find out what had happened to Luke's reckless animal.

Still Sophie was poised on the rail of the boat. *What's all the fuss?* she seemed to suggest with a superior flick of her slender tail. She studied the gap between the boat and the shore, stepping over the hands of anxious passengers who tried to restrain her.

On the jetty, Hannah was too busy wrapping a dripping, shivering Sinbad in somebody's spare sweatshirt to notice what Sophie was up to.

'Hannah, watch out!' Helen called from the shore. 'The crazy cat's about to jump!'

Her cry sent panic through the passengers on the ferry. The nearest lunged to grab the lithe cream and black animal, who kept her balance perfectly as the boat rocked hard.

Watch me! She leaned out from the slippery rail, using her tail as a rudder, getting ready to perform the return leap on to the jetty.

'Wow!' came the cries as Sophie crouched then leaped.

'Oh-uh-oh!' as she misjudged the distance.

Splash! Then silence.

'Not again!' Helen muttered. She waded back into the water for rescue number two, and did a flat-out belly-flop towards the spot where Sophie had gone in.

The passengers leaned over the side of the boat,

urgently pointing out the Siamese cat's bobbing head.

'Quick, before she sinks!' Hannah called. She held fast to Sinbad who wriggled inside the sweatshirt.

Helen did a clumsy crawl towards Sophie. She could see her black face and blue eyes bobbing on the surface. Why wasn't she sinking to the bottom like Sinbad?

'Hang on!' Hannah stood on the edge of the jetty, watching the cat's front legs paddle furiously. Her brown eyes opened wide and she gasped. 'Helen, you're never going to believe this!'

'What?' She gulped a mouthful of water as she spoke, thrashing her arms in and out of the water without seeming to make much progress towards Sophie.

'She might not need you after all.' The Siamese cat was making good headway towards the jetty. Her little face was tilted back in the water, her blue eyes were half closed. 'It's OK, you can stop!' she shouted at Helen as her splashing limbs threatened to swamp the cat. 'Sophie can swim!'

'. . . Of course, she can swim,' Helen muttered. The

excitement was over. Sophie had easily made it to the jetty and Hannah had leaned out to scoop her out of the water. Both cats were back on dry land and the ferry-boat had set off at last. 'Wouldn't you just know it?'

'Sorry!' Hannah giggled. Her sister stood on the jetty. Her hair was plastered to her head, her T-shirt and shorts dripped, and she was beginning to shiver.

Snuggled inside a borrowed towel, Sophie already looked warm and dry.

'We'd better get these two back home,' Hannah decided. She held Sinbad under one arm, and Sophie under the other. 'Then Dad can drive us up to Home Farm so we can get a change of clothes for you.'

'What's Miss Wesley going to say?' Helen wrung out the bottom of her T-shirt and flicked water from her eyelashes. Her bare feet made prints along the jetty as people in the queue made way for them to pass.

'Here she comes now.' Hannah saw their teacher's small, slim figure approach along the beach. She must have heard the hullaballoo from Lakeside Cottage, discovered the cause and come running.

'Oh, thank you!' she cried, seizing a bedraggled Sinbad from Hannah. 'Whatever got into you; you silly, silly boy?' She hugged Sinbad with tears of relief in her big grey eyes.

'It wasn't his fault,' Helen explained. She said a silent *ouch*! as Hannah stepped on her bare foot. 'What?' she hissed out of the corner of her mouth.

'Don't go blaming Sophie!' Hannah muttered under her breath.

In any case, Miss Wesley was so grateful to have Sinbad back safe and sound that she skipped the dramatic details. 'Let that be a lesson to you!' she told him, hugging him close. 'And don't ever go near that nasty lake again!'

'What Sophie needs is a toy!' Hannah declared.

She and Helen had told Luke all about the morning's fun and games as they sat in his garden at the back of the shop. Helen had borrowed an outsize white T-shirt belonging to Luke. It came down to her knees, and her skinny brown legs sticking out from the bottom still had goosebumps from her dip in the lake.

'What kind of a toy?' Luke asked. He shook his

head at his adventurous pet as she climbed on to his lap and rubbed her face against his chest.

'Something to keep her occupied, so she doesn't go wandering off and getting into mischief.'

'Good idea,' David Moore agreed. He sat back in a deck-chair, soaking up the sun.

'You can teach Siamese cats to fetch a ball!' Luke brightened as he lifted Sophie and stood up. 'The only problem is, we don't have one.'

'Try a rolled-up sock,' Helen suggested. She didn't know if it would work, but it was worth a try.

So Luke fetched a white cricket sock from inside the house and soon the twins were crawling across the lawn, training Sophie to fetch it back when they threw it for her.

'Bring it!' Hannah cried, as she rolled the sock along the grass.

Sophie chased it and batted it with her front paws. She drew back and pounced, dribbled it and dived for it, but she didn't bring it back.

'Hmm.' Helen frowned and thought again. 'I've got a better idea.'

She asked Luke if he had a wire coat-hanger and a piece of string, and while he went to fetch it, she found a strong stick which she stuck into the lawn so that it stood upright. 'We've got to unbend the wire,' she explained to Hannah when Luke brought the hanger, 'then twist it into the shape of a long arm. We fix the wire to the stick, so it juts straight out, see?'

Hannah helped her. 'Do we use the string to tie the sock-ball to the end of the wire?'

Helen nodded. 'The ball hangs down. Sophie comes along and bats it with her paw. It swings about, she bats it again, and so on.'

'Brilliant!' Their dad looked at the finished article. 'That should keep her happy for hours.'

Hannah tapped the ball to make it swing. Sophie watched it, ears pricked, front paws kneading the ground. She stretched up a paw to try it. The ball jumped away from her then shot back and hit her in the face. She rolled and jumped up, tried again.

'Excellent!' Luke said to the beaming twins. 'Do you think it's safe to leave her here while we go inside and find ourselves a long, ice-cold drink?'

They tiptoed away, watching over their shoulders as Sophie played with her fascinating new toy. She dipped and dived, leaped and rolled, while the home-made ball dangled and swung.

'Peace at last!' Luke sighed, handing out the lemonade in the cool of the kitchen.

'*Yee-owwl*!' The familiar cry came from somewhere inside the room.

Hannah shot a glance through the window out into the garden. It was empty. The toy swung gently to and fro.

Helen looked round the kitchen. She saw a movement between the folds of the white curtains, a flash of cream and dark grey, the blink of a blue eye.

'*Yee-owwl*!'

So much for a toy to keep her happy! Helen sighed.

Sophie clawed her way up the curtain, swung on to the smooth wooden pole, then stared down with what looked for all the world like a pleased grin and a tilt of her sweet head that seemed to say, *How's that for a balancing trick*?

Five

'Since you saw Luke yesterday morning, Sophie has climbed inside the fridge, broken two vases, and tried to chew an electric cable,' Carrie Lawson, Luke's sister from Crackpot Farm reported. It was late on Monday afternoon and she was manning the shop while Luke went off to roll his beloved cricket pitch as smooth and flat as velvet.

'Has she played with her toy?' Helen asked.

'No. I'm afraid it's not half as exciting as wrecking the house.'

A smile played about Carrie's mouth, but Hannah and Helen knew the situation was growing serious.

How could Luke make his home Sophie-proof when the cat was so agile and mischievous?

'Where is she now?' Hannah dropped her heavy school-bag by the shop door and looked nervously at the top shelf where Luke stacked his jars of sweets.

'She was last seen sunning herself on the front window-sill,' Carrie reported. 'Wasn't she there when you came in?'

Helen gave way to another customer who had just entered the shop. It was Dan Stott with his baby son, Joe. The tall farmer seemed to take up half the space in the tiny room. 'Did you just see a Siamese cat?' she asked him.

'Let's see now.' Dan gave it some thought. 'No, I can't say that we did. Why?'

'It's Sophie, Luke's new rescue cat from Stonelea,' Carrie told him. 'She looks as if butter wouldn't melt in her mouth, but that's far from the truth of the matter.' She launched into a list of the tricks that Sophie had got up to since she arrived.

'. . . Chased other cats . . . broken a jar of jelly-babies . . . fallen into the lake.' Helen and Hannah backed out of the shop on to the pavement to avoid the long catalogue of Sophie's crimes.

'Watch it!' Sam Lawson, Carrie's fair-haired, ten-year-old son, stood in their way. His head was tilted back and his hand shaded his eyes against the sun as he stared up at the roof of Luke's house.

'Sam, do you know where Sophie . . . ?' Hannah's voice tailed off. She followed his gaze on to the moss-covered, sloping roof. The cat stared back at her from the gutter. 'What's she doing up there?'

'Don't ask!' Helen took in the situation with one swift glance. 'Cat on roof. Doves in dovecote. Cat stalks doves across roof. Doves don't see cat . . . Chaos!'

Hannah realised she was right. Luke kept a dozen or so pure white doves in a new wooden house fixed to the wall at the side of his shop. There were small arched entrances for the birds to use and a ledge for them to roost on. Three sat there now, chests puffed out, tails fanned wide, gently cooing.

'Sophie, don't you dare!' Helen used a warning voice.

The cat turned her head to gaze at the doves. She spotted two more perched on the ridge of the roof, and one on the chimney pot. Her tail twitched. This definitely looked like fun.

'Sophie, if you don't come down this minute . . .' Hannah began.

'You'll do what?' Sam asked. As far as he could see, there was nothing the twins could do to stop the cat from chasing the doves. 'Anyway, she probably won't catch one. They'll fly off when they see her coming.'

'You don't know Sophie,' Helen warned. If any cat could successfully creep up on a bird, this one could.

And sure enough, she crouched low and began to make her way slowly and silently up the roof. 'The stealth of a leopard,' Helen murmured, imagining the jungle cat stalking its prey. Meanwhile, the three doves on the roof preened themselves, blissfully unaware.

'What shall we do?' Hannah whispered. It was natural for a cat to stalk birds, but she didn't want Sophie to catch one of the doves.

'Easy!' Sam came up with an instant solution. He clapped his hands noisily, then jumped up and down, waving his arms above his head. 'Scoot!' he yelled. 'Go on, scram!'

The birds spread their wings and flew off, rising with a flurry and curving off towards the safe cover of the beech tree. Sophie froze in mid-stride, halfway up the roof.

Sam shrugged. 'See. Nothing to it.' He picked his bike up from the pavement and slung his leg over the crossbar, ready to ride off.

'Except the cat's still on the roof,' Helen pointed out. 'And she's making her way up to the very top!'

Undeterred by the flight of the birds, Sophie had once more begun to pick her way across the slate tiles towards the chimney stack. Surefooted as ever, she reached the ridge and crouched quietly in the angle between the roof and the chimney.

'Make way there!' a cross voice called. It was Mr Winter, the ex-headteacher at Doveton Junior, and his ancient Cairn terrier, Puppy. 'Don't you know that bicycles aren't allowed on pavements?'

Mumbling under his breath, Sam moved out of the way. 'Bye, Mum!' he called to Carrie Lawson, then set off towards Doveton Fell before Mr Winter had a chance to tell him off again.

'Hannah, would you hold Puppy for me while I

go into the shop to buy some bread?' the old man asked Helen.

'I'm Helen,' she pointed out, knowing that it wouldn't make the slightest difference. She took the dog's lead and stooped to stroke his shaggy fawn head.

'And Helen,' he said to Hannah, beaming at her from behind his bristly white moustache, 'I hear you're the heroine of the hour. Wasn't it you who jumped into the lake yesterday to save Miss Wesley's cat?'

Hannah blushed. 'I'm Hannah.'

'Yes, quite. Well, anyway, look after Puppy between you. I won't be long.' He gave way to Dan and Joe Stott, who were on their way out, then disappeared inside the shop.

'Found your cat, did you?' Dan said in his low, easy-going voice. He followed the direction of Helen and Hannah's gaze to where Sophie still crouched by the chimney stack, head down, tail tucked round her body.

'*Pussy-dat*!' Joe said, pointing his chubby finger.

'On top of the roof!' Dan agreed. 'High, high up!'

Too high! Hannah said to herself. It seemed ages

since Sophie had moved from the spot. 'What if she's stuck?' she whispered to Helen.

'Don't joke!' Helen held tight to Puppy's lead.

'I'm not. Look how far she is from the ground. And cats do get stranded, you know! People have to call the RSPCA or the fire brigade. They climb up ladders to bring starving cats down from trees and roofs!'

'Typical!' Helen felt dizzy, even just looking up at Sophie. And it was true, she did seem fixed to the spot, as if she was too frightened to move. Meanwhile, the doves gathered on the dovecote ledge or flew idly from branch to branch in the nearby tree.

'You could try tempting her down,' Dan suggested as he headed for his Land Rover with Joe. 'Food. That usually does the trick.'

'Crisps!' Helen and Hannah decided at once.

Hannah ran inside to buy some cheese and onion flavour crisps from Carrie, then quickly brought them out to try Dan's idea.

'Crackle the packet,' Helen told her. 'Make sure Sophie can hear you open them.'

'Nice crisps!' Hannah called, wafting them

towards the roof. 'Your favourite!'

Sophie stayed stock still by the chimney, crouching there without so much as blinking an eyelid.

'Here, puss, puss, puss!' Hannah cried, standing on the bench to get closer to the cat.

'Hmph!' Mr Winter came out of the shop and saw what they were up to. 'That'll never work,' he told them shortly, taking Puppy's lead from Helen and stomping off down the Main Street. 'Try squirting water at it. A wet cat always comes down!'

'A wet cat . . . ?' Hannah echoed.

'. . . Comes down?' Helen frowned and wondered how on earth Mr Winter expected them to squirt water at Sophie.

'That's cruel.' Hannah decided against it. 'Anyway, knowing Sophie, you could drench her and she still wouldn't shift.'

'So what?' Helen's neck began to get a crick from staring up at the chimney stack.

'So, I'll climb up and fetch her!' It was the only way. True, it was a long way up, and true Hannah wasn't very fond of heights. But what else could they do?

'Are you sure?' Helen stepped back for a better view. 'I suppose you could get up on to that lean-to bit at the side of the house, and from there on to the higher bit.'

Hannah nodded. 'It's not a very steep slope. I think I can manage it.' If not, Sophie could be stuck on the roof overnight.

'Better take the crisps with you.' Helen shoved them towards her and Hannah stuffed the packet down the front of her school jumper. 'Once you get near enough, try offering her one again. This time she might be tempted.'

So Hannah edged along the bench and stepped from it on to the shop window-sill. From here she could haul herself on to the lean-to section of the roof.

'Careful!' Helen warned, as the bench wobbled.

Hannah's feet were on the sill, she was reaching up and holding on to a water-pipe, heaving herself up.

'*Yee-owwl*!' Sophie saw the top of Hannah's dark head appear. Her eyes shone a brilliant blue from the dark shadow cast by the chimney stack.

Clumsily Hannah pulled herself on to the lower

part of the roof. She glanced down, then closed her eyes. *Bad mistake*! she told herself.

'Are you OK?' From below, Helen could only see a pair of legs sticking over the edge.

'Fine,' Hannah said in a breathless, wavery voice. She looked up again. What had seemed an easy climb from ground level now looked impossible. She lay flat and began to edge her way forward.

'That's it, you're nearly there!' Helen urged, though in fact there was still miles to go.

'Who's nearly where?' Carrie Lawson came out of the shop and looked up. 'Hannah Moore, come down at once!'

Her loud voice startled the doves in the dovecote and sent them flapping clear of the house. Sophie gave a loud cry which died away to a growl. She glared down at Hannah and shifted further into the shadow.

'Hannah, if you fall, whatever will I tell your mother and father?' Carrie clasped her hands to her chest.

'Don't worry, she's OK,' Helen assured her. 'Sophie's stuck on the roof. Hannah's going to rescue her.'

'B-but . . . !' Mrs Lawson was lost for words. She saw Sophie shuffle against the chimney stack, looking this way and that at the birds as they wheeled overhead. 'That cat's not stuck!'

Clinging to the roof, Hannah heard the words. Not stuck? What then?

'She's hiding from the doves,' Carrie Lawson told them in a slow, patient voice. 'Playing a waiting game, hoping that they'll forget she's there and land close by.'

'You mean she can get down any time she wants?' Helen gasped. 'Are you sure?'

'Of course. A gentle slope like that is no problem for her. She could do it with her eyes closed.'

'Oh no!' Hannah groaned and laid her face flat against the smooth, warm slates. All this for nothing.

'In fact, she looks pretty mad with us for scaring the birds away.' Mrs Lawson had got over her surprise and stood with her arms folded. She watched the doves flutter and settle at a safe distance.

Sophie followed their flight with her eyes, watching their every movement.

'Come down, Hannah.' Helen admitted that Sam's

mum was right and that they'd jumped to the wrong conclusion.

'Easier said than done.' Hannah gritted her teeth and glanced down. Climbing up had been difficult, but getting down was going to be even worse.

'I'll fetch a stepladder from Luke's store-room,' Carrie said, and vanished inside.

'Hang on!' Helen told Hannah, as calmly as she could. She saw Sophie creep out of the shadow of the chimney, tail twitching, padding surefootedly along the ridge. And there, at the far end of the roof was a single, cheeky dove. The bird pecked and

preened, chest puffed out, choosing to ignore all the recent disruptions to its afternoon routine. 'Uh-oh!' she muttered. 'Don't look now, but I think Sophie is just about to prove us wrong and Mrs Lawson right!'

Sure enough, the stealthy cat crouched and edged closer to the unsuspecting bird. Hannah saw them out of the corner of her eye, but she couldn't do anything, not while she was stranded, spreadeagled against the low roof. The palms of her hands felt sticky, her knees had begun to knock.

Inch by inch Sophie drew nearer to the dove. The bird dipped its beak deep into its chest feathers, *peck-peck*. Its beady eye flicked this way and that.

Pounce! The cat made her move. She launched herself, claws out, grabbing for her prey. In the nick of time, the bird spotted her. With a flutter of white feathers and a wild squawk she rose from the roof. Sophie landed a split-second too late.

'Ouch!' Down on the pavement, Helen closed her eyes. When she opened them, she saw Carrie come out with the ladder and set it against the lean-to roof, just in time for Hannah, who had lost her hold and come slithering down.

Bump-bump-bump. Hannah hit the rough edges of the slates. She felt her feet shoot over the edge, was aware of a rush of cream and black fur as a frustrated Sophie gave up the chase. 'Hey!' she cried, grabbing at the gutter as she slid. The ungrateful cat had just run her over.

Helen saw Hannah come to a painful halt. She saw Sophie speed down the roof, streamlined and elegant as ever. 'Uh!' she gasped, as the cat galloped over a helpless, flattened Hannah. Swift and lithe, she bounded on to the ladder, and from there on to Carrie Lawson's shoulder, where she braked and balanced perfectly.

Helen hid her head in her hands. 'Showing off as usual!' she groaned.

Six

'So, Luke, do you still think that Siamese cats make brilliant family pets?' Mary Moore asked the shopkeeper with a twinkle in her eye.

It was Friday evening, the night before the big cricket match, and Luke had called at Home Farm to discuss tactics with Helen and Hannah's dad.

'So loving and affectionate!' Helen teased.

'So very, very clever!' Hannah added. She was still stiff and sore from her adventure on the roof earlier in the week. When she'd eventually managed to climb down the ladder, she'd reached firm ground with a packet of crushed crisps stuffed down her jumper and her hands and knees covered in grazes.

Luke sighed and cleared his throat. 'Er, let's just say that it's taking me longer than I expected to teach her the basic rules.'

'Like how to stop climbing into fridges and up curtains,' David Moore laughed. 'Or chasing doves, or breaking vases and wrecking your shop!'

Sophie's reputation was spreading. The whole of Doveton knew about her escapades.

'Give me cuddly, cosy Socks any day!' Helen tickled the tabby cat under the chin.

Socks purred and rubbed his striped head against her hand. He lapped up attention, going from Helen to Hannah, then on to Luke to be stroked and petted.

'I still say you can't choose between a cat like Socks and one like Sophie.' Despite everything that had happened, Hannah wouldn't take sides. 'And when you think about it, they both have something in common.'

'Like what?' Helen couldn't see it. Sophie was slim and elegant. Socks was chunky. Sophie was strange and exotic. Socks was – well, ordinary.

'They both had cruel owners who dumped them.' Hannah's reminder made them all pause. When

Socks was a kitten, the twins had discovered him abandoned in the litter bin outside Luke's shop. He'd been scared and hungry, crying out for help. It was Helen and Hannah who'd brought him to Home Farm and nursed him back to health.

'You mean, the horrible man in Nesfield who left Sophie to starve?' Mary Moore picked up the thread. 'Yes, I suppose that does make me feel sorry for the poor little thing.'

'In any case, I keep hoping that Sophie will settle down soon.' Luke looked on the bright side. Then he collared David to talk about next day's match. 'We've got to hammer out a decent tactic to beat their chap, Dennis,' he insisted. 'Our best batsmen are Len Coates and Geoffrey Saunders. And we've got a good bowler in Dan Stott. Between us, we should give the Nesfield lot a good run for their money. And if we win tomorrow, we go top of the league,' Luke pointed out. 'It's a really vital match.'

'Don't remind me.' The twins' dad frowned. 'The big question is, if Dennis tampers with the ball again, like we suspect he did last time, will our batsmen be ready to deal with it?'

Hannah and Helen overheard the urgent

discussion without paying much attention. They were getting ready to saddle Solo and meet Laura Saunders and Sultan down at the Manor. Speckle was to come with them on their ride by the lake. So they came and went, in and out of the kitchen, fetching hard-hats, boots, bridle and bit, while the men planned and plotted how best to defeat the rival team.

'I think we should talk it over with Geoffrey Saunders,' their dad said suddenly. He stood up, ready for action. 'He's our best hope of hitting lots of runs, but we ought to warn him what he might be up against.'

'Now?' Mary asked. She looked at her watch to see that it was six o'clock. 'Do you mind if I come too? I fancy a chat with Valerie in their beautiful, peaceful garden.'

'That means we're all going to the Manor,' Helen pointed out. She had Speckle on the lead. Hannah was at the door, already mounted on Solo. 'See you there!'

It was a warm evening. White clouds drifted over the tops of the fells, a slight breeze rippled the surface of Doveton Lake as Hannah rode Solo along the shore.

Helen threw a stick for Speckle far out into the water. It broke the surface with a splash as Speckle charged and swam furiously towards it. Laura's chestnut horse skittered sideways, hooves clattering on the pebbles.

'Whoa!' Laura urged. She coaxed the big horse back into line and together he and Solo walked gently on.

Speckle reached the floating stick and grabbed it between his jaws. He swam back and came out of the water, his black coat streaming.

'Speckle, no!' Helen cried. She saw the dog's head go down as he dropped the stick and prepared to shake himself dry.

Speckle ignored her warning. A shower of water drops spread far and wide, soaking her from head to foot.

Laura and Hannah laughed from a safe distance. The dog barked for the stick to be thrown once more, but Helen resisted. 'You'll only drench me all over again!' she complained. It was time to get back to Doveton Manor.

'Here, it's your turn.' Hannah slid easily from the saddle and handed her Solo's reins. She gave Helen a leg up and grabbed the bike that lay nearby. 'Maybe Mum and Dad and Luke will still be at your place,' she said to Laura, cycling off over the bumpy pebbles.

The Manor stood at the far end of the village, set back from the road. Tall stone gate-posts led down a long drive flanked by smooth lawns, up broad steps to a grand house surrounded by rose-terraces, statues and ponds. Sultan's paddock lay to one side. Around the back were the stables and the yard where the Saunders parked their cars.

'. . . Expect the ball to bounce awkwardly . . . it could swerve at the last minute . . . be prepared.' The voices of Luke Martin and David Moore could be heard urging Doveton's best batsman to be on his guard.

'I'll do my best,' Geoffrey Saunders promised. He sounded determined to defeat the crooked bowler. 'If there's one thing I can't stand, it's someone who cheats!'

Laura, Hannah and Helen rode by the terrace with Speckle in tow. The sun was beginning to settle over distant Rydal Fell, but there was still plenty of time to help Laura unsaddle Sultan and brush him down before the twins set off for Home Farm.

They were in the stable yard, unbuckling the girth strap and fetching brushes and combs from the tack-room when a loud cry pierced the air.

'*Yeeowwl*!'

It came from the direction of the fish pond; a screeching, unmistakable wail.

Highly-strung Sultan tossed his head and reared up. Even steady Solo flared his nostrils and pulled at his tether. Speckle cringed low, head between his paws.

Hannah stared at Helen over the chestnut's broad shoulders. 'Sophie?' she whispered.

'It can't be!' Helen trembled at the idea that Luke's cat had found her way in amongst the Saunders' prize goldfish in the pond.

'Don't worry, it's only Lady,' Laura assured them. She went ahead and unsaddled her horse.

Lady was the Saunders' own pedigree Siamese cat. She lived a life of luxury among the plump cushions and soft rugs of the splendid living-rooms, or sunning herself amongst the flower pots on the wide terraces.

'*Yeeowwuhh*!' A second cry went up.

'Hang on a moment!' Half way across the yard with the saddle slung over her shoulder, Laura stopped. '*That's* Lady!'

'So who was the first one?' Helen scrunched up her face and shuddered, knowing the answer without being told.

'I knew it. It's Sophie!' Hannah hissed.

'By the fish-pond!' Helen gasped.

'About to have a fight!' Laura concluded.

The warning yowls had turned to fierce spitting and hissing. Claws must be out, teeth bared.

'Laura, see if you can sort out that racket,' Val Saunders called from the sunny spot round the side of the house where the grown-ups were sitting.

'And watch out for my koi-carp!' her father reminded her. 'Don't let those cats get anywhere near!'

So the three girls left Speckle with the horses and ran to the pond. Sure enough, the two Siamese cats stood face to face in the shadow of a stone cherub overlooking Mr Saunders' pond. The little angel was one of a pair, both with smiling faces, curly hair and tiny stone wings.

'Which one is which?' Hannah asked. To her, the two hissing cats looked identical.

'That one's Lady. Her face is lighter. She's a Blue Point.' Laura picked out her own cat straight away. 'Look, we've got to move fast, before they start tearing each other's eyes out!'

Helen nodded. 'We'll close in with a sort of pincer movement, you on one side, Hannah and me on the other.' She crouched behind another, taller statue, ready to move forward.

Laura agreed. 'When we get close enough, we each try to grab a cat. Let's hope they're too busy to notice us.'

'*Waa-agh*!' Lady opened her mouth wide and howled. Her delicate ears were laid flat against her head, her tail carving through the air to warn the intruder off.

Sophie arched her back and spat.

'*Waagh*!' Lady darted her head forward. She swished the air with her paw.

Just in time, Sophie dodged the dangerous claws.

69

'Phew!' Hannah edged after Helen. 'That was close.'

'Maybe Sophie's met her match at last,' Helen muttered.

Ten metres away, along the other arm of the pincer movement, Laura was creeping on her hands and knees between huge pots of geraniums. Her fair ponytail hung forward over one shoulder, her immaculate jodhpurs were getting grimy, but she seemed not to care. All that mattered was to stop the fight between the two angry cats.

'*Yee-owwl!*' Sophie bared her teeth and howled louder than ever. With one leap she was up on the stone cherub's head, spitting down at her rival.

'Maybe not!' Hannah sighed.

Sophie's cheeky move had made Lady furious. Straight away she bounded on to the head of the matching cherub and eyeballed the stranger. The two cats perched on the stone heads, above two carved, ever-smiling faces.

Hannah and Helen crawled slowly forward. At the far side of the pond, Laura crouched ready.

'Now!' Laura cried at last. A few seconds more and it would be too late. Limbs would

be locked in battle, fur would be flying.

Helen jumped up and snatched at Sophie. Laura made a grab for Lady.

Sophie nipped smartly off the cherub's head on to the stone border of the fish-pond. Lady darted clean through Laura's arms and made off across the terrace, between the flower-pots, heading for the house.

'Get Sophie!' Helen gasped at Hannah. She'd overbalanced against the cherub and made him wobble. Now she had to steady him while Hannah went after Luke's cat.

Hannah held her breath. Sophie stalked along the rim of the pond, flicking the end of her tail, surprised but satisfied that she seemed to have seen Lady off. Now the garden was all hers. She prowled confidently on, round the pond, glancing down at the half-dozen fat, lazy carp swimming amongst the lily pads.

'Quick, Hannah!' Laura cried.

They heard grown-up feet coming along the terrace to investigate; saw Sophie put her head to one side, test the water with her paw and consider her chances of landing one of the expensive fish . . .

'Oh no you . . .' Hannah whispered. She made her lunge. '. . . Do-on't!'

Her hands met thin air. She was toppling forwards and Sophie had jumped clear.

One bound across the pond, and the cat was streaking up the terrace after Lady.

But she, Hannah, had stubbed her toe against the stone ledge. She was falling forwards, towards the smooth shining surface of Mr Saunders' pond, towards the white, cup-shaped lilies and the flat green leaves as big as dinner plates. The goggle-eyed orange fish stared up at her.

Splash! Helen gasped in horror as this time Hannah hit the water face-first.

Seven

'My koi-carp!' Geoffrey Saunders hared around the corner of the manor house, long legs leaping over flower pots and swerving between statues. Close on his heels came Valerie Saunders and David and Mary Moore.

From the direction of the yard, Speckle bounded towards Hannah who sat amongst the lily-pads, waist-deep in the fish-pond. He jumped right in beside her, tugging at her T-shirt to pull her out.

'Down, Speckle!' Helen tried to haul him back. She saw flashes of salmon-pink, orange and white as the costly fish flicked their tails and tried to hide under the leaves at the far side of the pond.

'Get me out of here!' Hannah wailed. She pulled a long, slimy weed from her hair and spat out the taste of pond water from the gulp she'd taken as she'd landed.

'What on earth's going on?' David Moore stood, hands on hips, as Helen gave Hannah her hand and pulled. A faint smile played on his lips as he watched Speckle carry on trying to rescue an ungrateful girl.

Water streamed from the legs of Hannah's jeans as she stepped shakily out of the pond. 'Lady and

Sophie were fighting!' she explained. She glared at Helen for daring to break out into a grin. 'They were!' she insisted, spitting and spluttering, squelching her trainers across the stone-flagged terrace.

'That's quite right, dear. We heard them,' Valerie Saunders said soothingly. 'And accidents will happen, however careful you try to be.'

'. . . Four, five, six!' Mr Saunders was busy counting his fish.

It reminded Helen of a fire-practice at school, when you stood in line in the playground and answered to your name as the teacher called it out.

'. . . Seven . . . eight . . . nine!' He grew more anxious, searching under nearby shrubs to see whether any of the poor fish had spilled out of the pond as Hannah had fallen in.

Valerie Saunders took Hannah by the arm. 'Come into the house with me,' she suggested. 'I'll find some spare clothes of Laura's for you to change into.'

Squelch-squelch-squelch; Hannah trailed after her across the terrace.

'. . . Ten!' Mr Saunders muttered.

His voice faded as Hannah and Mrs Saunders went

round the corner, through the yard towards the kitchen door.

'At least you broke up what could have been a very nasty fight,' Laura's polite, refined mother was too good mannered to complain about the trouble Hannah was putting her to. 'Where exactly did Lady and Sophie go afterwards?'

'Erm, towards the house.' Hannah stood dripping on the doorstep, waiting there for a set of dry clothes.

'Both of them?' Val Saunders called from the laundry room, a tinge of surprise in her voice.

'I think so. Lady went inside through a french-window. I'm not exactly sure what happened to Sophie.'

'Will a T-shirt and shorts do for now?'

'Yes, thanks.' Hannah listened to cupboard doors being opened and closed.

'Oh my goodness!' Mrs Saunders' well-bred voice rose to a small shriek. 'Oh, Hannah, come here and look!'

With a small jolt of dread, she trotted across the tiled kitchen floor, *squelch-squelch*, into the small laundry room lined with shelves, washing-machine and drier. 'What is it?'

'Up there!' Laura's mother pointed to a sunny shelf by the window. Two Siamese cats lay side by side on a soft, warm towel. They licked their front paws with their rough pink tongues, then wiped their faces clean. They licked again and went round the backs of their ears, shaking their heads and murmuring softly. Grooming time. They made firm strokes with their delicate paws. And when the paler, Blue Point cat had finished her own grooming, she started in on the younger Seal Point. Lick-lick went her tongue, all over the darker cat's face.

'Lady!' Mrs Saunders breathed as her own fussy pet showed the visitor what being clean really meant.

'Sophie!' Hannah said in stunned surprise. For Luke's high-spirited cat sat and took it meekly. She lifted her chin obediently for bossy Lady to groom her neck.

'Whatever next?' Valerie Saunders wondered, handing Hannah her change of clothes, and going off smiling with astonishment to tell the others.

'At least we're even,' Helen grinned. It was Saturday morning, and so far all the grown-ups had been too busy thinking about 'The Match' to pay much attention to the knotty problem of Sophie the show-off. At that very moment, their dad was upstairs getting ready.

'*How cumb?*' Hannah spoke through a blocked nose. Her dip in the Saunders' fish pond had left her with a cold.

'Looking after Sophie has given us both a soaking we didn't expect.'

'Huh. You can say *dat* again.' Hannah was folding their dad's cricket trousers, shirt and pullover, then putting them into a hold-all.

Helen packed the sandwiches and buns that the twins and their mum had made before she went to work. They were the teams' refreshments for that afternoon's needle-match. 'Not changing your mind about Sophie, are you?' She couldn't resist a sly dig at her sister.

Hannah zipped the bag and sighed. '*Doh. Whedever she does subdig dat bakes be bad, I just say "Bister Lewis" to byself, and dat rebinds be dot to be cross.*'

Helen stared. 'Oh, I see. Whenever Sophie does something that makes you mad, you just say "Mr

Lewis" to yourself, and that reminds you not to be cross?'

'*Yeb. Dat's what I said*!' Hannah sniffed and took the bag out to the car. '*Dad's ebber so dervous*,' she whispered to Helen, in case he heard through the bedroom window.

'Ever so nervous?' Helen repeated as she stacked the food tins on the back seat.

'*Yeb. Why do you keeb on rebeating ebberydig I say?*'

Helen grinned at Speckle and Socks, who sat at the door. She changed the subject. 'I bet even these two realise that today's match is special.' There was excitement in the air, building up every time their dad rushed through the kitchen looking for his cricket boots or phoning Luke to check the time he should arrive.

'*Batch ob de Day*!' Hannah agreed.

Match of the Day. '*Dah-de-de-de-duh-duh, Dah-dah-de-de-de-dum*!' Helen sang. She was looking forward to it, even though it meant leaving Speckle at home. 'You be a good dog,' she said softly, as she led him to his comfy basket in the kitchen and watched Socks curl up beside him.

'Ready?' David Moore dashed through the room, looking for a hairbrush.

'Ages ago,' Helen said calmly.

'*Be doo*,' Hannah added.

' "Me too"!' Helen interpreted. She watched him find the brush in the hall and run it quickly through his unruly brown hair. 'Will you want us to help you and Luke work on the pitch, or shall we put the sandwiches and cakes on plates in the pavilion, ready for the interval?'

'Sandwiches, please,' their dad decided.

'*Clig-filb*!' Hannah said, as if she'd suddenly remembered.

'What?' For once even Helen was stumped.

'*Clig-filb*.' She went to the drawer and pulled out a packet of cling-film. '*To cober de blates.*'

David Moore stared hopelessly at Hannah and shrugged. He took one last look around the house, reached for his keys and shooed them out. 'Let's go!'

'*Dah-de-de-de-duh-duh*!' The twins sang the TV theme tune all the way down Doveton Fell to the smooth green expanse of the village cricket pitch. It was the one thing Hannah could say without Helen having to translate.

* * *

'How's your nose?' Helen asked. She was putting rows of plastic cups along the counter in the cricket pavilion.

'*A bid bedder.*' Hannah blew into her tissue and spoke again. 'A bit better. There!' She sat on the verandah step, keeping away from the food in case she spread germs. Instead, she was idly watching their dad and Luke push the heavy roller up and down the wicket.

'Only an hour to go,' Helen said. At one o'clock, the teams would begin to arrive. Setting out the cups was her last job before she went to join Hannah outside. 'You'd think they would've rolled that pitch smooth enough by now,' she sighed.

'I *doh* . . .' Another loud blow into her tissue. '. . . I know! But it's this Dennis *de* Menace they keep worrying about. They have to be able to prove he's cheating, and one *thig* – thing – that'll help is to have the ground *ber* – perfectly level.' Out of the corner of her eye Hannah saw Mr Winter's shiny blazer buttons wink in the sun as he strolled round the boundary of the pitch.

'Oh no!' Helen groaned as she saw him too. He'd

brought Puppy along, and the wheezy little terrier was poking about in the hedge bottom as his master stopped to watch Luke and David at work. 'All we need is a telling off from Mr Winter!' Even if they hadn't done anything wrong, this was what he was bound to do.

' "Helen, why aren't you in school? Hannah, why aren't you doing something useful instead of sitting around all day?" ' Hannah mimicked the ex-headteacher.

Luckily for them, he stood, arms clasped behind him, supervising the rolling of the pitch.

'Hey!' Luke looked up and caught sight of Puppy. 'Don't let that dog anywhere near my wicket!'

'It's quite all right,' Mr Winter assured him in a loud, calm voice. 'Puppy knows he mustn't go on the pitch.'

'Hmm.' Luke rolled up his sleeves and nodded at David Moore. 'One last time!' he said.

As the two men turned the roller and set off down the central strip of grass, Helen and Hannah caught another movement across the pitch. It was a sleek shape gliding under a fence, trotting along the far boundary; a cream animal with black legs, tail and face.

'Guess who!' Hannah and Helen said in the same breath.

'Sophie?' Luke suddenly stopped pushing at the heavy roller, leaving the twins' dad to stagger on alone. He'd spotted his naughty pet lurking by the fence. 'I thought I'd left you safely asleep in your basket!'

His voice attracted Puppy's attention. Now the terrier saw the cat. He yapped and set off across the smooth green grass.

'Puppy, come here at once!' Mr Winter shouted.

No way. Dog sees cat. Dog chases cat. Helen realised that the old teacher was wasting his time.

Puppy's barrel-shaped body bounded across the pitch, his stumpy tail pointed straight up, his ears pricked and his black eyes gleaming behind his mop of cream hair.

Sophie stopped and gave him an aloof stare.

'Puppy!' His owner set off after him at a creaky, old man's pace.

'Uh-oh, let's go!' Helen said to Hannah. 'You head Puppy off. I'll try and catch Sophie.'

So Hannah got up and sprinted for the disobedient terrier. In no time she'd cut across his path and, before he had a chance to set foot on Luke's precious central wicket, she steered him back the way he'd come.

Yap-yap! Puppy protested loudly but he soon gave up. In any case, the width of a whole cricket field was a long way for his fat little legs to run. And the Siamese cat looked pretty nimble.

'Bad dog!' Mr Winter scolded, standing in Puppy's path, legs wide apart. The terrier scuttled right through them and ran on towards the gate.

Meanwhile, Helen thought fast. *Salmon sandwich*! She grabbed one from a plate on the counter and sprinted from the pavilion towards the cat. Even Sophie wouldn't be able to resist the lure of fish.

'Here, there's a good puss!' She slowed down as she drew near. Sophie's little nose was twitching. She'd smelt the salmon.

'Come and taste it.' Helen dropped to her knees and held out the sandwich. She saw Sophie turn and stretch her head towards the food, take one step then another. Her pink tongue curled around her top lip. Slowly, blue eyes gleaming, she came within reach.

Wait until she actually takes a bite! Helen held her breath. Sure enough, the juicy salmon between slices of brown bread was irresistible. Sophie opened her mouth and sank her teeth into the sandwich.

Helen swept her up into her arms.

She heard Hannah clap and her dad shout well done. As Sophie struggled, then changed her mind and tucked into the rest of the salmon sandwich, she yelled across at Luke. 'What do I do now?'

'Take her home for me and shut her in the kitchen,' he shouted back. 'And listen, Helen, don't take any chances. Once this match gets underway, the last thing we want is for Sophie to get loose yet again!'

Eight

'It's a lovely day for it!' Dan Stott called as he strode towards the pavilion, cricket bag in hand.

Luke and David waved back. They were putting the very final touches to the pitch.

The sun was shining, light clouds floated high in the bright blue sky.

'Hello, you two,' the tall farmer said to Hannah and Helen, stopping on the pavilion step.

'Hi, Mr Stott. Is Joe coming to watch the match?' Helen asked eagerly.

He laughed. 'He's only a toddler, remember. What would he know about cricket?'

'About as much as us,' Hannah grinned. She felt she would never get the hang of the rules. Maiden overs, googlies and off-spinners, legs-before-wicket; they were all terms that baffled her.

'Well, as a matter of fact, Joe is coming down later with Julie. A lot of the wives are going to be here to cheer us on. With a good home crowd behind us, I reckon we've got a real chance of pulling this off.'

'You'll go top of the league, if you do,' Helen reminded him. She saw other Doveton players drive into the small car park and head for the pavilion; Len Coates from Skrike Farm, Mark, the gardener from the Manor, and the upright figure of Geoffrey Saunders himself.

'Don't mention fish!' Hannah muttered under her breath. Though Mr Saunders hadn't lost any of his precious koi-carp when she'd landed in his pond, she still wasn't sure that he'd forgiven her.

Helen giggled.

'Fish?' Dan queried, in a voice loud enough for Geoffrey Saunders to hear.

Laura's father gave Hannah a dark look and strode past them into the changing-room.

'Take no notice,' Helen advised. 'Everyone knows it was all Sophie's fault.' She took a quick look round the ground to make sure that the cat hadn't got out of the house again and followed her. She'd been extra careful to follow Luke's instructions and carry her home. She'd told Carrie Lawson that it was important to keep Sophie inside for the whole of the afternoon.

Luke's sister had been minding the shop. 'Let's put her in the living-room.' She'd collared Sam and told him to make sure that the windows and doors were shut so that the cat couldn't get out. Then she'd promised Helen that she would keep an eye on her.

'What are you looking for now?' Hannah asked, as more Doveton players turned up. On the wooden verandah of the pavilion, the early arrivals had already got changed and were now earnestly discussing their tactics for the match.

'Nothing. Just checking,' Helen said casually. There was no sign of Sophie over by the fence, or by the gate that led out on to the main street. But her heart did sink a little as she recognised the stiff, white-haired figure in the dark blue blazer that had just arrived. 'Mr Winter!' she warned Hannah.

'Ah, Helen, Hannah; just the people I wanted to see!' The old headteacher spotted them from a distance. He bellowed and beckoned them to join him.

'Bad luck. Better jump to it.' Luke grinned at the twins as he and their dad finally finished work on the pitch and came to get changed.

'What's he want?' Hannah said through gritted teeth.

'He probably wants you to help him keep score,' David said. 'That's Mr Winter's regular job, whenever we have a home match. You see that hut over there?' He pointed to a tiny wooden shed without windows by the fence where Sophie had strayed earlier in the day.

Helen and Hannah nodded glumly.

'That's the scorer's hut. Mr Winter sits inside and keeps track of the number of overs bowled and runs scored. He needs someone to hang the giant numbers on the hooks on the outside of the hut so that the crowd knows the score.' David Moore described their fate. 'Sam Lawson usually gets press-ganged into doing the job, but he doesn't seem to be around today.'

'I don't blame him,' Helen grunted. What could be more boring than hours spent hanging numbers on hooks?

'Do your duty, girls.' Luke insisted that it was an important job.

'Helen-Hannah!' the crusty old man shouted, waving both arms.

So they left the bustling pavilion and trailed across the ground after Mr Winter, who showed them how a large flap on the front of the scorer's hut lifted up and was propped open on long metal rods.

'As official scorer, I sit inside with a clip-board, pen and paper,' he explained briskly, then showed them a pile of giant white numbers. 'Here are the number-boards. There are the hooks you hang them on whenever I tell you to change the score.'

Helen sighed. 'This is worse than being at school!' she whispered.

'*I thig by cold suddenly got worse*!' Hannah snuffled.

Helen glared at her. 'Don't you dare!' Hannah had to stay with her to listen to Mr Winter's long, boring explanation of their duties.

'This is the hook to indicate number of overs . . . This hook is to show last man out . . . This hook . . .'

Hannah stifled a yawn and let her gaze wander towards the car park at the far side of the ground. Half a dozen cars had just pulled in and a group of men she didn't recognise were stepping out.

'Here comes the Nesfield team!' Helen suddenly brightened. Things were beginning to liven up at last. The gang of strangers set off towards the pavilion, laughing and joking amongst themselves.

Hannah nodded. Mr Winter's voice droned on, but she and Helen could sense the mounting tension as the Doveton players stepped to one side to let the visitors into the changing-room.

'See that big one with the dark moustache?' Helen picked one player from the Nesfield team; as tall as Dan Stott, but much broader, bringing up the rear of the visiting group. He was suntanned and walked with a swagger, as if he expected everyone to get out of his way. 'I bet that's Dennis!'

Hannah agreed. She disliked the man on sight; the way he held his head high so that he looked down his nose at the gathering crowd, the sneering set of his mouth beneath the thick moustache.

'Hannah-Helen, are you paying attention?' Mr
Winter broke off from his description of their duties.
He frowned and pushed in between them. 'Ah, I
see; our opponents have arrived.' He nodded
knowledgeably. 'They have some first-class players
in their side. Our boys will have their work cut out
to beat them today.'

As the Nesfield team filed inside to get changed,
Hannah dropped Mr Winter a quick question to
confirm her and Helen's suspicions. 'Which one is
their main bowler?'

'Let me see.' Taking a pair of glasses from his top

pocket, the old teacher settled them on his nose. 'Ah yes; that would be the chap with the moustache. Apparently he lives abroad for part of the year; I expect that's why he has such a good tan. His name's Dennis Lewis.'

Hannah nodded. Dennis the Menace. She and Helen had guessed right.

'Dennis who?' Helen frowned and stared at the burly man by the pavilion door.

'Lewis,' Mr Winter said briskly, going inside his hut to set out his clip-board, pencil and paper.

Hannah and Helen's mouths fell open. *Lewis . . . Nesfield . . . a house in Spain*! They recalled the details of Lucy Carlton's sad story of Sood Sawaat Chaem Choi.

'That's him!' Hannah gasped.

Lewis let his gaze roam around the ground, taking in the gathering crowd, the perfectly prepared wicket, the boundary hedges and fences.

Helen took a deep breath to swallow back her anger. Just the sort she'd imagined; a know-it-all and a cheat. 'That's him all right.'

Dennis Lewis, the cruel owner who'd left Sophie to die.

Nine

The Doveton team won the toss and Luke, their captain, put Nesfield in to bat. Dan Stott, their best bowler, soon sent the wickets tumbling.

'Five down, five more to go!' Helen kept careful count of the number of Nesfield batsmen still to come.

'That's a total of 85 runs so far,' Mr Winter said from inside his hut. He leaned out to speak to the twins. 'Is the scoreboard correct?'

Hannah nodded. It was hard to concentrate. She kept thinking about Dennis Lewis, and picturing what it would be like if someone were to leave him alone in an empty flat without food for weeks on end. All through the Nesfield innings she wondered how she would react when it came to his turn to bat.

'Here he comes!' Helen hissed.

They watched Lewis clump out of the pavilion, bat tucked under his arms, walking awkwardly in the thick pads strapped around his shins. He wore a navy blue cap with a wide peak, which he pulled down over his eyes as he took up position at the wicket.

'Get him, Dan!' Hannah whispered. She longed for Lewis to be out for a duck.

Their friend from Clover Farm polished the leather ball, ready to begin his run-up. He ambled towards the smooth wicket, then picked up speed, whirling his arm over his head to release the ball. It shot like a cannon-ball straight at Lewis.

Bounce-thwack! The bat hit the leather. Lewis whacked the ball low and fast. Luke dived to stop it and missed. It sped all the way to David Moore on the boundary. Meanwhile, Lewis and his fellow-batsman made two runs.

'87 runs!' Mr Winter said from inside the hut.

'Huh!' Helen put the new number on to the board.

Dan wiped the grass from the ball and tried again. Lewis faced him with a confident sneer, cap pulled well down, lining himself up to send the ball for six this time.

'Miss it!' Helen prayed, as Lewis swiped at the bullet-like ball.

Crack! The batsman caught the ball in the middle of his bat and sent it flying. Two more runs, then none off the next ball, then two more. By the last ball of Lewis's first over, it was clear he meant business.

Dan Stott ran the back of his hand across his forehead to wipe off the sweat. He would have one more shot at Lewis before he gave way to another bowler. Polishing carefully, taking his time, he ran up to the crease and unleashed the ball.

Whack! Lewis swung out wildly. He caught the ball badly and sent it skywards, up . . . up . . . up.

'Catch!' Hannah whispered, as the ball soared towards their dad.

David Moore ran under it, squinting up at the sun. There wasn't a sound from the crowd as the ball dropped towards his cupped hands. Thud! It landed safe and sound.

'Hurrah! Brilliant catch! Well done, David!' There was loud applause. Hannah and Helen jumped up and down and hugged one another. Their dad had got Dennis Lewis out at the end of his first over!

'91 for 6!' Mr Winter declared. He ticked boxes and wrote down numbers. 'That was a fine catch,' he told Helen and Hannah. 'A very fine catch.'

'Dad's a hero!' Hannah cried, enjoying every moment of seeing the angry batsman stomp off the pitch.

'BUT!' Mr Winter broke into their celebrations. 'Don't get carried away just yet.'

'Why not?' Helen was already ready to celebrate victory.

The old teacher tutted and shook his head, ready to begin scoring again as the next batsman came on to the field. 'If I'm any judge, that catch of your father's will only serve to fire Dennis Lewis up. When it comes to his turn to bowl, you may be sure that he'll be dead set on getting his own back!'

Nesfield's batsmen were all out for 132 runs. Helen and Hannah clocked up the final score, then made their way to the pavilion for orange juice and sandwiches.

'133 to win,' Luke was telling the Doveton team, who gathered round to hear their captain talk. 'That's not too high a target to beat.'

'So long as they play fair,' Geoffrey Saunders said in a low voice.

The Nesfield team huddled and muttered in another corner of the pavilion, anxiously talking tactics.

'It'll be grand to go top of the league!' Len Coates looked forward to victory. He was first man in, with Geoffrey Saunders, and was already strapping on his pads and testing out his batting strokes.

Meanwhile, Hannah and Helen stared hard at Dennis Lewis. He'd broken away from his team and gone to speak to a group of smart, tanned women sitting on the grass by the verandah. They were Nesfield supporters and evidently great fans.

'We know you can bowl this lot out, no problem,' one woman said, smiling up at him from her deck chair.

'I'll do my best,' he said smugly, standing hands in pockets, swaggering for their benefit.

'I expect you have a few little tricks up your sleeve as usual!' Another one smiled knowingly.

'Shh!' the first one said. She'd caught the twins staring at their group.

'Aren't they Mary Moore's girls?' a third woman whispered. 'You know; the woman who runs The Curlew.'

'Oh yes, the animal-loving identical twins!' The first one didn't even try to keep her voice down. After all, these were only children they were discussing so rudely.

The whole group smiled at Helen and Hannah in a superior way. The third woman smirked and turned back to Dennis. 'Haven't you heard about Home Farm since they took it over? They've filled the place with animals they've rescued – stray cats and dogs, ponies – you name it, they've got it!'

Helen fumed and was about to stalk off, but Hannah tugged her arm and held her back. 'Listen!' she warned.

'Animal-lovers aren't exactly your sort of people, are they, Dennis?' The second woman thought the whole thing was a great joke; talking about people in a loud voice without a care over who heard.

The burly cricketer shrugged, but said nothing.

'Oh yes, they are, he's one himself!' the third woman contradicted. She tipped her sunglasses on to the top of her head and looked up at him. 'A little birdie told me that you'd bought yourself a cat earlier this year!'

Hannah stared. Her brown eyes flashed angrily from the women to Lewis.

'Not me,' he grunted. He turned rapidly with an angry frown, and went to join his team.

'What did I say to upset him?' the woman protested, eyes wide, eyelashes fluttering.

The other two sighed and tutted, said she certainly

knew how to put her foot in it.

'No, really!' She spread her manicured hands wide. 'I'm sure I heard that Dennis had bought a cat. One of those strange-looking ones with a peculiar miaow. A Siamese!'

'*Howzat*!' Lewis flung both hands in the air and made an appeal to the umpire.

'Not out,' the man in the white coat replied calmly.

Doveton were 26 for no wickets. Geoffrey Saunders and Len Coates had settled solidly into their innings.

Lewis dropped dramatically to the ground, slapping the grass with his palms.

'Did you see that?' Hannah screwed up her eyes and stared from her position by the scorer's hut as the bowler got up and prepared to bowl the next ball.

'I saw him grab a handful of grass and dirt,' Helen said.

'Exactly.' Hannah knew what this meant. 'Lewis will slip the dirt into his pocket and use it to rub on the ball when the umpires aren't looking!'

'It'll make the ball bounce all wrong,' Helen agreed. 'And make it difficult for our batsmen to hit.'

'If only we could do something!' Hannah watched Lewis thunder down the pitch and make a fierce delivery to Geoffrey Saunders. The ball kept low and shot under the bat. It struck Mr Saunders on the foot in front of the wicket.

'*Howzat*!' The roar from the Nesfield team went up again.

This time the umpire gave Mr Saunders out. The twins saw Luke and their dad shake their heads and get into a little huddle with Dan Stott, as Laura's dad let his head drop and walked off. There was no arguing with the umpire; when he gave 'out', that was it.

'Not fair!' Helen grimaced. In spite of Luke's careful work on the pitch, it still seemed that the umpires didn't suspect Lewis of cheating.

'Not fair!' Hannah said again, when Len Coates's wicket fell to another swerving, skidding ball.

And 'Not fair!' they said together, with the score at 109 for 9. Dan Stott had just been given 'out' to one of Dennis Lewis's noisy, bullying appeals. Now there was only Luke and their dad left to bat, and still 24 runs to be made.

At last Luke went up to one of the two umpires and spoke quickly and urgently.

'He's telling him about the ball tampering!' Hannah crossed her fingers and hoped that he would listen. There was no doubt about it; Lewis deserved to be sent off for cheating.

But the umpire shook his head. He stood solidly behind the wicket and waited for David Moore to take up his place at the crease.

'Dad and Luke can do it!' Helen promised herself. After all, 24 runs didn't seem so very much.

Mr Winter sat, pen poised, inside his hut. 'We only have three overs left to play,' he reminded them.

Hannah did the sum in her head. Six balls per over. 'Three overs equals eighteen balls. That means they have to score fours or sixes to give us any chance of winning!'

'They can do it!' Helen watched Dennis Lewis square up to the man who'd caught him out during his own innings. She saw him dip secretly into his pocket and draw out a handful of dirt. 'Cheat!' she muttered savagely.

David Moore tapped the ground with his bat, then stood ready. He used every grain of concentration in his body.

Lewis thundered towards the wicket. The ball flew from his hand, hit the grass and skidded low.

Chuck! David made contact. The ball sped low past the fielders towards the boundary.

'Four runs!' The umpire signalled to the scorer.

'Yes!' Hannah raised her fist in a salute. 'Brilliant, Dad!'

'Do it again!' Helen cried. She hooked a one and a three on to the score-board to make it read 113.

115 ... 120 ... 125. Luke and David played beautiful cricket and piled on the runs.

'*Howzat*!' Dennis Lewis threw himself red-faced at the umpire, desperate to get the last man out. There was one over left to play. Six balls and eight runs to be made.

'Not out,' the umpire said without blinking.

'Come on, Dad, come on, Luke. You can do it!' Helen and Hannah whispered. They backed up against Mr Winter's hut and held their breaths as the bowling changed ends.

'The result is on a knife-edge,' the old teacher

told them. 'It can go either way!'

'We know!' they sighed, closing their eyes, hardly able to look.

Thwack! The crowd roared as David hit another four runs.

129. Helen brought the score board up to date. Only four runs needed.

Lewis trod heavily towards his mark, hand in pocket, secretly drawing out the treacherous dirt.

'Watch out, Dad!' Hannah yelled a warning.

David nodded and stood ready. As the ball bounced and swerved, he was able to get his bat to it in the nick of time. But there was no run scored. Four runs off four balls. It was still possible.

Yee-owl! A quiet, scarcely audible cry drew Helen and Hannah's attention away from the tense finish. It came from somewhere close by, above their heads. Their hearts almost stopped as they heard it and realised what it meant.

'Sophie!' Hannah whispered. *Not now! Not here!*

On the pitch, Lewis prepared to bowl again. David faced him, patting the ground nervously with his bat.

'Where is she?' Helen cried. Stepping out of the

shade of the hut, she turned and looked up.

A face stared down from the roof; an elegant, aristocratic, wedge-shaped face with blue eyes and long white whiskers. A slim neck stretched out, two front paws edged forwards.

'Sophie, no!' Helen hissed.

Above their heads, the cat got ready to jump.

Ten

Hannah stared up at Sophie. She glanced over her shoulder to see Lewis thundering down the pitch to deliver the third ball of the final over.

Chuck! David Moore nicked the ball solidly between the fielders. He made one run off it as the crowd yelled and cheered him on.

'130!' Mr Winter said from inside the hut, furiously ticking boxes.

Hannah changed the numbers as Helen pleaded with the runaway cat. 'Stay there!' she murmured. 'Just for a little while. The match is almost over. We can win!'

Sophie flicked the end of her long, kinked tail. '*Yeeowwl*!' she said, louder this time. She teetered on the edge, judging the distance from the roof to the ground.

'Don't even think about it!' Hannah ordered, as sternly as she could.

The Siamese cat leaped daintily. She landed on the smooth, clipped grass at Hannah's feet, her blue eyes fixed on the two figures in white who sprinted between the wickets.

'131!' Mr Winter cried, his voice strangled with excitement. 'One ball left. We need two runs to win!'

Sophie swished and sashayed in front of the scorer's hut, attracting the attention of one or two spectators. She lifted her paws in a playful little dance, fell on to her side and rolled, sprang to her feet again.

'Watch out, there's a cat loose on the pitch!' someone in the crowd cried.

'Grab her!' Helen hissed to Hannah. In the centre of the cricket ground, she knew Lewis was winding himself up to deliver the final, deciding ball to her dad.

'Here, Sophie!' Hannah decided on stealth, not force. She dropped to her knees and put out her hand, danced her fingers along the ground. 'Come and play!'

The cat stretched out her paw to tap Hannah's hand. She put her head to one side and considered the game. *Boring*! she decided. Instead, she leaped straight up, twisted in mid-air and shot off across the pitch.

'Oh no!' Helen could hardly bear to look.

The cat sped gracefully towards the wicket where the real action was. She swerved between the fielders, long tail streaming behind her, ears laid flat as she bounded on.

Lewis pounded down the field for his last delivery. David Moore faced him. Neither man had seen the cat. *Whizz*! The bowler unleashed a cannonball of a bowl. *Thwack*! David swung out and hit hard. The ball shot from his bat.

'Run!' the crowd yelled.

The twins' dad left his crease and charged to change ends with Luke.

Good fun! Sophie liked this sort of game. She scooted between David Moore's legs as he ran.

'Ooh!' the crowd gasped as the batsman almost tripped and fell.

'Aah!' A sigh of relief as he regained his balance and ran on.

Luke and David scored a run and turned to charge back along the wicket.

'One more run needed!' Mr Winter dashed out of his hut and jumped up and down. The crowd roared the batsmen on.

'Throw me the ball!' Lewis yelled, waving his arms at the fielder who had scooped it up. 'Come on, I can stump him if you get a move on!'

The fielder launched the ball through the air. It soared towards an impatient Lewis as Luke and David ran on.

Great game! Sophie thought, showing off and racing Luke this time. She streaked alongside her breathless owner, tangling herself between his legs.

'No!' Hannah groaned. The cat was about to lose them the match.

But Sophie surprised them. Suddenly she broke free of Luke. She bounded sideways out of his path and did one of her miraculous back-flips. Landing with the grace of a gymnast, she shot off again, this

time towards the burly figure of Dennis Lewis.

The crooked bowler ran backwards into position to catch the fielder's throw. He didn't see the cat. Sophie flew towards him, saw him tottering back, arms outstretched. She aimed between his legs and slipped through as he stood ready to catch. At the split second that mattered, Lewis noticed the cat flash by and took his eye off the ball. It fell with a thud to the ground.

'He missed it!' the crowd gasped. Then, 'Run, Luke! Run!'

Luke reached the crease as Lewis scrabbled on the grass for the dropped ball.

'133 runs!' Mr Winter threw his arms in the air.

Helen and Hannah jumped up and down and hugged. 'We did it!' they yelled. 'We won!'

David and Luke were the heroes of the match. The Doveton team gathered round and slapped them on the back, the crowd cheered as they walked back to the pavilion.

Helen and Hannah cheered loudest of all. They forgave Sophie on the spot, gathered her up in their arms when she trotted meekly back towards the hut and smothered her in strokes and kisses.

'Don't ever do that again!' Hannah tried to scold her for showing off and running on to the pitch, but she cuddled and squeezed her close, unable to be cross.

'What if Dennis Lewis complains to the umpire about Sophie getting in his way?' Helen wondered. She could see the big, sulky figure hanging back behind the others. He'd taken defeat badly, flinging the ball to the ground and scowling darkly.

'He'd better not!' Mr Winter stepped in between them. 'If he does, I'll have a word or two of my own to say about certain illegal uses of the cricket ball!'

Hannah and Helen stared at the old teacher in astonishment. He must be talking about the dirt that Lewis had secretly used. 'You knew?' Helen stuttered.

Mr Winter raised his bushy white eyebrows. 'I had my suspicions before the match. And today I've seen quite enough to confirm them as correct.'

'Why didn't you say something?' Hannah still hugged Sophie, who snuggled cosily against her.

'One doesn't like to openly accuse a chap of

cheating,' the ex-headteacher said stiffly. He set off determinedly across the pitch, flinging a final word over his shoulder. 'But you can be sure that a quiet word from me in the umpire's ear will definitely stop Lewis from using the same dirty trick in future!'

'Wait!' Helen had a sudden idea. She ran after the old man and quickly told him the story of how Dennis Lewis had abandoned the very cat who had just won the match for Doveton.

'. . . Sood Sawaat Chaem Choi,' she told him, her eyes blazing, her heart beating fast. 'She's a pedigree cat. Her name means Dearest Sweet Lady in Thailand.'

'Disgraceful!' Mr Winter's eyebrows met in the middle in a deep frown. Like Helen and Hannah, he was an animal lover who couldn't bear to hear tales of cruelty and neglect. 'I suppose the police were called in and Lewis received a proper punishment?'

Helen shook her head. 'He was living in Spain at the time. It was in February this year. Miss Carlton said that the police couldn't do anything.'

'But he's back now!' Mr Winter pointed out the obvious. He fumed and fretted. 'Someone should tell the police. The man should be prosecuted!'

Helen nodded. She knew she didn't need to say any more.

The old headteacher narrowed his eyes thoughtfully. 'As a matter of fact, I have a friend in the Nesfield police force. Inspector Frank Jennings . . .'

Helen nodded again, and gave Hannah a small thumbs-up. Mr Winter was a useful person to know.

'What I'll do is give him a ring and drop the hint that the owner involved in the cruelty case earlier this year has returned home. I'm sure Inspector Jennings will be most interested and willing to take up the case again . . .' Mr Winter thought it through.

'Thank you!' Helen gave a big sigh. The old teacher could be trusted to bring Lewis to justice in more ways than one. Smiling happily, she let him go to speak with one of the umpires while she went to tell Hannah the good news.

'Thank you . . . thank you!' David Moore took the crowd's praise modestly. He grinned, took off his cap and ran a hand through his untidy hair. Slowly he worked his way through to the peace and quiet of the pavilion. Then he propped his bat against the wall and turned to wait for Luke, Helen, Hannah and Sophie.

'What's it like having a dad who's a sporting hero?' Luke unstrapped his pads and laid them on the bench.

'Great!' Helen's eyes shone, a smile split her face from ear to ear.

'And you!' Hannah reminded Luke. 'You're a hero too!' She was still catching her breath after the final thrilling moments of the match.

Outside, the crowd was beginning to break up. People headed for their cars, proud that Doveton had gone top of the league.

'Let's not get too big-headed,' Luke said, pleased but shy. 'If anyone's the real hero, it has to be Sophie!'

The Siamese cat squirmed in Hannah's arms. 'Did you hear that?' Hannah giggled. For the first time in her life, Sophie was being praised for showing off.

'*Yee-owwl*!' she said.

Helen's hands flew to her ears.

'You may be noisy,' Hannah went on. 'And you may be the most terrible show-off, getting into mischief everywhere you go . . . !'

Sophie blinked her enormous blue eyes then wriggled free. She landed silently on the floor and prowled across to the counter where the remains of the cricketers' tea was still spread out.

'BUT?' Helen knew there was a great big 'but' in Hannah's sentence. She grinned at her dad and Luke.

'BUT . . . !'

Sophie jumped smoothly on to the table. Snaffle went her delicate jaws over a squashed cream bun. The cream splurged out of the sides and spread over her face. A delighted Sophie began to lick it off with her rough pink tongue.

'But in spite of everything . . .'

'*Everything*?' Helen interrupted. Everything included luring Sinbad on to the Doveton Belle, stalking Luke's doves, fighting Lady by the Saunders' fish pond . . . and that was only half of it!

'In spite of everything,' Hannah insisted. She laughed at Sophie's sweet, black, cream-covered face. 'We love you, Sophie. We really do!'

STANLEY THE TROUBLEMAKER
Home Farm Twins Summer Special

Jenny Oldfield

Meet Helen and Hannah. They're identical twins – and mad about the animals on their Lake District farm!

Stanley's a champion hamster and he's favourite to win the Doveton Summer Show. But behind the scenes, rival owners are plotting, and when Stanley escapes from his cage just before judging begins, Helen and Hannah suspect someone's let him out on purpose. The twins vow to find him – but Stanley's not so keen to be found . . .

HOME FARM TWINS
Jenny Oldfield

66127 5	Speckle The Stray	£3.50	❑
66128 3	Sinbad The Runaway	£3.50	❑
66129 1	Solo The Homeless	£3.50	❑
66130 5	Susie The Orphan	£3.50	❑
66131 3	Spike The Tramp	£3.50	❑
66132 1	Snip and Snap The Truants	£3.50	❑
68990 0	Sunny The Hero	£3.50	❑
68991 9	Socks The Survivor	£3.50	❑
68992 7	Stevie The Rebel	£3.50	❑
68993 5	Samson The Giant	£3.50	❑
69983 3	Sultan The Patient	£3.50	❑
69984 1	Sorrel The Substitute	£3.50	❑
69985 X	Skye The Champion	£3.50	❑
69986 8	Sugar and Spice The Pickpockets	£3.50	❑

ANIMAL ALERT SERIES
Jenny Oldfield

All Hodder Children's books are available at your local bookshop, or can be ordered direct from the publisher. Just tick the titles you would like and complete the details below. Prices and availability are subject to change without prior notice.

Please enclose a cheque or postal order made payable to *Bookpoint Ltd*, and send to: Hodder Children's Books, 39 Milton Park, Abingdon, OXON OX14 4TD, UK. Email Address: orders@bookpoint.co.uk

If you would prefer to pay by credit card, our call centre team would be delighted to take your order by telephone. Our direct line *01235 400414* (lines open 9.00 am–6.00 pm Monday to Saturday, 24 hour message answering service). Alternatively you can send a fax on *01235 400454.*

TITLE		FIRST NAME		SURNAME	

ADDRESS	
DAYTIME TEL:		POST CODE	

If you would prefer to pay by credit card, please complete:
Please debit my Visa/Access/Diner's Card/American Express (delete as applicable) card no:

Signature .... Expiry Date: ....

If you would NOT like to receive further information on our products please tick the box. ❑